THE SKALD

THE SKALD

SPEAR OF THE GODS
BOOK 0.5

GREGORY AMATO

Cover design by James T. Egan of Bookfly Design
Illustration by Blane Bellerud
Edited by LP Tvorik and Jess Lawrence

Paperback ISBN: 979-8-9880613-4-2

Sed Ferro Press
3439 NE Sandy Blvd, #484
Portland, OR 97232

CONTENTS

THE SKALD

CHAPTER 1

THE RAVEN'S ADVICE

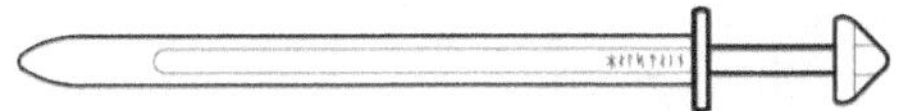

YOU CAN GET GOOD INFORMATION FROM ravens if you have the fresh eyeballs of your fallen enemies to trade. Ravens don't give information for free, of course. That wasn't the sort of payment I carried, though. Eyeballs are squishier to pack than the latest gossip and rather more difficult to extract in the first place. A story will get you the same information. Sometimes even better, if your story is good.

Ravens do love the eyes, though, and I wished I had some at that moment. The raven staring at me thought little of the story I offered.

"There are too many people in this story," said the raven in mumbly East Norse. "And it's too complicated. Nobody wants to sit through all that."

I didn't want to talk to this bird anymore. He was rude and his warbly eastern dialect made me want to plug my ears with rocks. But I needed his information.

I sat on a ridge overlooking a sea of pine trees at

the end of a steep slope down. New country for me. So far east it was practically the land of the Swedes, which would explain the bird's dialect. Behind me the sun shone, if on little but bare rock and lonely hills, and it would for a while yet given the long summer days. It had been an easy trek so far, and would be easy enough to go back over those same hills. But it was the landscape of failure if I walked back over it now, returning home without completing my delivery.

Shame was powerful in my world, and failure meant a lot of shame. My foster father Halstein would not yell or strike me if I told him I could not deliver the sword he'd forged. He would just nod heavily and think less of me. A few days later he would suggest I was better suited to milking cows and, knowing I hated milking cows and would refuse, would move on to other suggestions. Plying my trade as a skald with a jarl, perhaps, or joining a raiding crew.

Reasonable suggestions for a skald. And not to my liking at all. Pleasing or displeasing a jarl sounded like a lot of restriction and a lot of pressure. And I was no fighter to join a raiding crew. There was a lot of freedom in being a delivery man, and a lot of advantage in traveling with the skills a skald has.

For all the fear of finding a new line of work, it was the shame that most frightened me, pushing urgency past caution. The thought of having to endure a lessening in Halstein's mind after all he had taught me meant I had to find a way forward through those pines.

The right path forward. Daylight did not last forever, even in the summer, and the wrong path might be the last one I traveled.

Just my luck to have run into a discerning (to put it politely) raven named Judgment. What I would have given to be questioned by one of Odin's ravens instead. Thought and Memory both sounded preferable to Judgment.

Normally I could figure my own way forward on instinct or information from other travelers, with no help from a raven. But my instincts were screaming that avoiding danger would be like threading a needle here. Heavy mist hung over a broad valley thick with tall trees ahead of me. No going around it. That was one foreboding forest, and I knew my foreboding forests. How to choose my approach, then? That was what the raven would help with. Supposedly.

"Thorgrim killed Vestein because his wife made Vestein a shirt?" The bird shook his head, the blue sheen of his feathers catching the light. "That doesn't make any sense. Wait, I see." He cocked his head and drew back, confident he had seen through the veil of my story. "You humans say 'making a shirt' as a euphemism for something else!" *Aha!* said the raven's face, insofar as ravens can make faces.

Head in my mittened hands, I sighed into the frosty air and wondered if I was wasting good daylight. It had been a lonely trip and I had not picked up any new stories on the way, so I was using one I knew from Halstein himself. He had traveled from the west fjord lands and through more of Midgard than anyone I knew.

That was before I was born. After I was born, Halstein settled back where he had come from to foster me and to work his forge. He made weapons, I brought them to their new owners. So far, I had not failed a delivery. I rarely failed to earn my supper and a safe night's rest with my storytelling either, but this was not working out as planned.

"Are you crying?" demanded the raven.

"Shouldn't you stick to heckling Christians?" I quipped, sitting up straight before the bird could make up its own story about me. "I am laughing at you."

"Laughing at *me?!*" gasped the bird.

Sometimes, during my travels, I would find old, kindly ravens out in the nowhere parts of the world. The kind that would tell you stories just to have an audience, no trade involved. They tended to be on their last legs, looking for those few listeners before the end. I sometimes wondered if ravens were the spirits of long-dead skalds awakened in bird form. If true, this raven must have been a terrible skald.

"Laughing at you!" I shouted, my voice echoing out. My legs dangled over the edge as the ghosts of my words found their way down the rocky crags. Slopes here were steep and near impassable for most people, certainly for anyone not packing light and well prepared. I was not most people, and I did indeed pack light.

Working as a delivery man for the best blacksmith in Midgard had some benefits. For one, it meant excellent crampons, which helped me scale any incline my feet were willing to attempt. Scaling this one had left me in need of a rest, and that was when I had found the raven.

I had not anticipated a shouting match with a bird.

"Your story is terrible!" croaked the black-winged bastard. "No one cares who made a shirt for who. Bad stories like that aren't going to get you much. Where are you even going?"

"Folki's farm," I said. "Delivering a sword from Halstein in Dafvik."

"You should get better stories to trade for a trip that long. Maybe talk to a skald. They know all the stories."

"I am a skald. Ansgar the Skald."

"On-scar?"

Troll-cursed, unintelligible Swedish ravens. "ANSGAR. ANSGAR THE SKALD."

"Oh. Well. Well met."

Meeting a raven seemed a fortunate thing when I first ran across Judgment. You don't travel through Midgard's loneliest spaces, avoiding the main roads and many of the forests, because you expect chance company will be friendly. The roads often had bandits. The forests often had semi-nameable terrors I did not fancy running into.

Why semi-nameable? Because nobody lived long enough to fully describe them and come up with good names. If it was magical and malignant, it was a troll. If it was previously dead but sticking around like a bad guest, it might be a *draugr*, but that was just another kind of troll. I still had a fair distance to travel, and information from a sky-borne source sounded like my logical next step in determining the safest route ahead.

"I was giving you a story others would not have. You are just missing the implications. Wait a moment and let me explain."

Was I an experienced traveler ready for any weather and any terrain? Yes. Did I want to run smack into a pack of wargs, or worse, in the forest? No. And to improve my chances of not dying on this run, I needed to bite my tongue and take my foster mother's advice about making friends with such birds. Or, failing that, at least making them fair trading partners.

"It is no simple thing to weave a good shirt. Wives make shirts for their husbands, and we like to think the quality of the weave is indicative of the love a wife has for her husband."

"Is it?"

"It's more indicative of how much she has worked at a loom," I said, "but quality is not the point."

"What is the point then?"

I had forgotten that ravens didn't care much about human intrigue. If they can trade it, sure, but it doesn't grab their attention like killing. If I could only get a little farther, though, I was sure I could hook him.

"Intent! It is not normal for a woman to make another's husband a shirt. It is a show of affection, and that has—"

"Consequences!" gasped Judgment. The prospect of violence had picked up his interest. "What happened?"

"That one loose thread unravels the rest of the story. Thorkel overheard that his wife might have had feelings for Vestein, so Thorkel was angry and wanted to kill him."

"That makes sense," said Judgment. "Your people are rather insane. Suspicion is just as likely to have you all kill each other as evidence."

No argument there.

"But why are these other people involved?" he continued.

"Thorkel? Ah, he couldn't kill Vestein. For one, he was too lazy. A bit of a coal-biter. More likely to stay indoors than go outside and achieve anything. He also couldn't kill Vestein because Vestein was a close friend of his brother Gisli."

"Ah, so he wanted to protect his fragile ego by killing a man, but he didn't want his brother to be angry at him."

"Right."

"So this lazy Thorkel person with hurt feelings, what did he do?"

"He asked his friend Thorgrim to kill Vestein."

"A bold move. I suppose that is somewhat interesting." Judgment was playing down his interest, but a good skald knows his audience. And when your audience is a raven, murder narratives trade like fine silver.

"But we aren't even halfway done," I said with a flourish. "Thorgrim killed Vestein in secret. Only . . ."

". . . Only what?"

"Only he left his spear in Vestein's guts and Gisli pulled it out."

Judgment gasped as he flapped his wings. Esoteric as some of our traditions were, the raven knew this implication without me telling it. "So Gisli was honor-bound to take vengeance for the murder! But his own brother ordered it, so he's conflicted! What happened?"

"That's the last I heard," I said in a hushed tone. "But you know it's only going to escalate with both brothers fighting each other through proxies. It's got blood-feud written all over it. Who knows how many people will get themselves killed in the back and forth?"

"It's going to be a bloodbath! A real feast for ravens!"

I got to my feet slowly and dusted myself off. Judgment did a little dance and turned himself around, not realizing we were at the end of our game. "I am glad you agree it is a good story. Now tell me what's lurking nearby and how to avoid it."

Judgment's face fell a little. Like any good negotiator, the raven knew he ought to have downplayed the value of what he'd received, but I had caught him up in the excitement of humans killing each other. I didn't mention the events had probably taken place more than twenty years ago. Perhaps things had played out and the story had ended. Or maybe it had turned into multi-generational warfare. Family drama was about an even chance for that. Either way, I was done with my end of the bargain. There would be no denying reciprocity here. Ravens, much like spirits, had very transactional senses of fairness.

I didn't like that bird. I had known I wouldn't as soon as he gave me his name. But he was the only one in sight at the time, and I needed him. I had a sense that the information he gave me, about a pack of wargs to the south and a witch to the north, was incomplete. The witch was not the seeress kind, or he would have called her a *volva*. Instead, he called her a *roof-rider*, the kind of sorceress you might see flying at night, if you were very unfortunate. The kind that was more likely to use my manparts for rituals than to read my future.

He knew something of the forest but didn't have the full story. We would both have to get used to less satisfaction than we expected.

Due east was dangerous as well, but he still suggested going in that direction. It was a winding path, but I could find shelter with a friendly soul a few miles in.

"He says he's a farmer," said Judgment, "but, you know, there are a lot of dangerous things in that forest below, and I don't know what a farmer would farm there. Soooooooo . . ."

So, probably not a farmer. An old warrior or exiled nobleman if I was lucky. An outlaw or sorcerer if I wasn't. Even so, my chances were better with an outlaw or sorcerer than with the other residents of the forest. Running straight into a pack of man-eating wolves or a witch's curse meant almost certain death. Or worse.

Life lessons are sometimes difficult to come by. Here is one: if you find an old man in a floppy hat feeling quite at home surrounded by monstrous wolves and manpart-nabbing witches, you can bet that old man is the most dangerous one of the bunch.

<h1>Chapter 2</h1>

<h2>The Witch's Forest</h2>

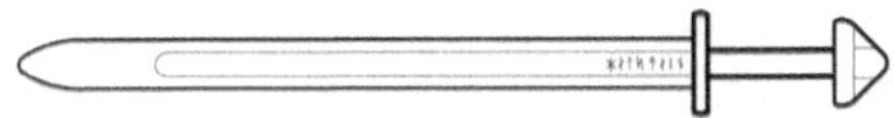

Down the steep hardscrabble was my best immediate way forward. Forward in the general sense. In a more specific and practical sense, I was going down, and fast.

"There's a path that winds down to the forest," Judgment told me.

"I've already got my crampons tied on," I said with a shrug.

That was true. What was *more* true was I wanted to show the bird up a little to ease the sting of being dependent on his advice. But *most* true, I was afraid of losing too much time and being caught in an unknown forest at night and having my eyeballs turned into Judgment's next breakfast. Unseen spirits like *landvættir* might favor me most of the time, but I was well beyond lands familiar to me. That meant unfamiliar spirits, and I could never tell if a place's particular *landvættir* would favor me or try to trip me up.

Climbing straight down was faster than any path

I might take. It was a steeper slope than the other side had been, and not easy with the weight of my pack threatening to take me off balance with each step. But I had learned to survive by climbing, running, skiing, and swimming faster and farther than anyone I knew in order to avoid having to fight my way out of a diffi-cult situation. The descent was well within my ability.

Judgment watched me from his perch above. "Unconventional," he announced after I had fin-ished, which almost sounded like praise. The raven waited until I was untying my crampons to dive out above me, coming to land a few feet away. "It's easier if I show you," he said, taking a spot on my shoulder once I was ready. "Go tree by tree. I'll point, and you go."

"These directions seem very specific."

"You could go the easy way if you had wings! But you just have stubby appendages instead, so I suggest you walk tree by tree to make sure you stay out of sight. The farmer lives deeper into the valley."

There was little point in winning the raven's ad-vice only to ignore it. I stopped at each tree, looking and listening, before moving on. Judgment was good on his word, and knew the quietest routes to take as I made my way deeper into the forest. His sense of danger was either uncanny or overstated. When he told me to low-crawl forward a while, I crawled. When he told me to hide behind a tree or a rock, I hid. It was during one of those times to hide I started to wonder if he was exaggerating the danger.

Eventually I had to peek. A woman stepped light as air and passed my face a mere arm's length away. Platinum hair wisped behind her in loose strands to reveal the smooth, pale skin of her neck. A light wool cloak billowed out behind her even though she was only moving at a fast walk and there was no noticeable breeze. The cloak's dark red exuded warmth, contrasting with the cool colors of her skin and hair. She held a distaff in her right hand, an ornate thing with a copper house set at its top.

It was only because her face was turned the opposite direction that I wasn't found out right there. She faced that way as if looking for something while she traveled. Maybe if I just waited I could see her face without her knowing. She seemed so young with that smooth skin. Perhaps—

Black feathers swatted the side of my face and brought me back to my senses. The reality of the danger rushed through me like a wave. I withdrew behind the tree and let her pass, holding my breath a good while before I dared move again.

"How have you survived this long?" whispered Judgment. "You are an idiot!"

"I thought you might be making it up to scare me," I said, feeling just as stupid as I sounded. "I've never encountered a witch that close before. A *vǫlva* or two, telling prophecies or healing people, sure, but never one I'd call a witch."

"I have never seen a man so easily baited by the sight of a young woman."

"She seemed so friendly. I mean, as I looked at her, that was the feeling I got."

"That is the trap! She'll lock your limbs if you meet her gaze. I'll leave your imagination to tell you what not-friendly things come after. Now shut up and follow me."

What gives the impression of sweet and nice is often the opposite. I hadn't forgotten that. It was common trope in myths and sagas. But there was a difference between thinking about it and experiencing that seductive pull. I was also a young man. Only nineteen winters. Older than that in lore. Younger when it came to women.

We took the path the witch had come from, hoping to put as much distance between us as possible. Soon after, I noticed a change to the forest. The pines I had seen from above were still there, swaying gently in the breeze far above me, but other trees I did not know began to appear.

My foster mother had done her best to hand down some basic woodcraft. I had spent more time thinking about her stories, and Halstein's poetry and languages. Now I regretted not paying better attention to the forest lore. The pines towered above, and here these thick but short trees grew bent in different directions. I touched one, and there was no give to the branch. It would not bend, and its bark resisted my fingernail without so much as a mark.

"What are these?" I asked the raven as I pointed to the strange trunks.

"You're a skald and you don't know?" he answered. "Those are ironwood. It's why this valley gets few visitors."

That made me shudder. I had always supposed the great forest called Ironwood, the one where Loki's spawn lived and propagated, was far enough away as to be unreachable. Not a place I could find even if I wanted to. Maybe just a story.

"We are far from that place," I said, shuddering and hoping what I said was true.

"Assuming it is just one place," said Judgment. "Maybe some of its denizens moved here."

"Then this is an even worse place than I thought!"

Judgment shrugged. "Maybe for you. Good place to find eyeballs to eat."

That did not make me feel better.

Another mile or so in and the ironwood trees grew taller and thicker, though no less bent in their attempts to grow skyward. Judgment bade me slow down as we approached a mound with one such tree so tall it looked like it had broken through to the sunlight above. No light streamed down from it. In fact the hill itself was somehow darker than everything around it.

"This way," said the raven as one big black wing slid across my vision.

"I can't see anything when you do that," I said.

"You won't see anything if you don't go where I tell you, either!"

Nobody likes being told what to do. Some people don't just dislike it, but deliberately seek out things they are not supposed to do. I was one of the latter. It was why I was so bad at herding sheep and why I thought I was so good delivering weapons out on my own. Sometimes when I tell my story, I shake my head in recalling the stupidities I engaged in. But the stupidities are as much a part of my history as the nobler parts.

"I want to see what's up there," I said, gesturing toward the mound, and about to engage in one of such stupidities.

"You don't!" said the raven, making me want to see it even more. "What happened the last time you ignored me?"

"There *was* a witch that time. She will be miles away at this point, and there is something strange about this mound."

Strange was not exactly the right word. It was eerie—still in a way that felt like the life around me held its breath. The kind of quiet that sounded less like nothing and more like death. It was not as if the *landvættir* were hiding in the rocks and earth and trees, eyeing me with hostile intent. It was as if they were not there.

"Bad idea," said Judgment.

A mound in another place might indicate a burial site. Not this one. Or if it was, it had survived an age or two to have a tree growing on it too thick for me to wrap my arms around. This was a strange valley indeed, almost like it was part Midgard and part Jotunheim. An in-between place, as my foster mother Taika had described once, a *Myrkviðr*. There was much lore to discover in forests like these if you could come out of them alive.

I also remember Halstein shaking his head at exploring such places. He had seen much of Midgard, but traveling among other realms was too much. Taika had seen less of Midgard, but often told me of other realms. Where she had wandered, or where she had sent her *hugr* out away from her body, I never found out. Here was an in-between place, it seemed to me. It would be shameful to return telling only how I hurried through it, my head down, afraid to explore it.

"I want to have a look. I think that mound has something interesting about it."

The raven shook his head. "Go investigate if you're having trouble imagining, then."

Whatever that meant.

Dead leaves covered the soft earth and smooth boulders pockmarking the mound. Careful as I chose my steps, there was a crunch each time that made me hold my breath. It seemed to take forever to ascend the mound even though it was probably a matter of seconds. I knocked on the trunk of the great tree and cut a knuckle on a bit of the bark.

I inhaled sharply as I sucked on my knuckle and that was when I smelled the blood. Not my blood, surely, since I had only a small scrape. You can't work on a farm and not come to know the iron-tinged smell of blood in quantity.

I glanced back at Judgment, who was half-hidden behind a tree. He was waving one wing and mouthing something. I could read lips a little bit, maybe. I certainly could not read beaks. I waved back and walked around the tree. I would be done exploring soon enough.

The corpse hung from its wrists, which were hammered onto the tree. The scents of iron and decay twisted together like two snakes spiraling upward. The man's intestines rotted in front of him, belying the expression he had died with. Blood sat in a basin at his feet, having run down from a cut on his right thigh.

In the basin was something else. I stepped closer to look, holding my nose and leaning in until I was only a foot away from the thing. Coarse fibers broke the surface and in a moment I realized what I was looking at. These were clothes soaking. A light and small garment, whatever it was. The dark red of the witch's cloak now seemed not so warm after all.

This was what the bird meant: he would leave it to my imagination to tell me what came after my limbs had been locked. Now I did not need to imagine.

There was no sign of Judgment when I looked up. But he had pointed the way, so I turned in that direction. I froze on my first step.

Just at the edge of my vision, a cloak of crimson wool billowed despite the lack of wind.

Don't look her in the eyes. Don't look her in the eyes. Don't look her in the eyes.

I ran, cursing myself for indulging my potentially fatal curiosity.

Behind me I heard high-pitched laughter. Amusement mixed with dismissal. She would enjoy the chase and had no doubt she would get the better of me.

Ahead, the forest closed in. The *landvættir* would not help me. The witch would be too powerful for them, or else they would already favor her. Branches moved in closer and struck my arms and shoulders, but I turned with them and kept going. Roots rose to trip me, but I hopped over.

The witch's sickly sweet voice beckoned me to stop and turn around, promising rest and food and 'womanly attentions' under a warm blanket. She giggled at that last promise. Judgment's advice steeled my heart against her influence. I kept running until there was what looked like a steep drop-off. A thick veil of white fog prevented me from seeing how steep. I could leap that and break a leg, or both. Or I could stop to check and allow the witch to catch me.

No time to make a decision, no way I would chance a look behind. I needed to chance the jump. If I could keep running after that, I might even be close enough to the farmer to find safety. How would I know if I couldn't see? Didn't matter. If I couldn't find my way, maybe I could lose her in the fog. If it came to it, I could fight, but that was a bad option. My seax required me to get too close, and my sling required me to look at my target.

I leapt into the fog. My feet looked for land longer than I had expected, and for a moment I thought my bowels might drop faster than I did. It was just a little too long, maybe no more than a few inches, but the sensation of nothing is a terrifying thing when you expect solid earth beneath you. I stumbled when I finally made impact with soft ground and was lucky to keep my footing. I had penetrated that wall of mist and survived. Maybe my luck would hold after all.

After another minute of running at full speed, the world had gone completely white and I was afraid to deviate from my direction, even to lose my pursuer. So on I went, my heart hammering in my chest as much from fear as from exertion.

Judgment's direction proved true when the outline of a house appeared no more than a stone's throw in front of me. Thick fog sat everywhere but right outside the entrance to the house, and so I could not see how far the structure stretched. I headed straight for the door and banged and yelled, polite and desperate at the same time.

"Ooooo-OOOOO-ooooo . . ." The witch sang behind me, somewhere out of sight. Each note varied its pitch and, somehow, seemed to change the direction it was coming from.

She was stalking me, waiting for my fear to build before she struck. It was working.

No one stirred inside. I would need to fight. At least I had a structure to my back as I turned to face my pursuer. I was not good at fighting, sure, but Halstein had at least drilled a few basic lessons into my head. The first was to keep my back against something solid to avoid being taken from behind.

I thought of him as I drew my seax, also of his making, and tried to steady my breathing. It was my first knife, too big for me when I was young but a fine tool and weapon as I grew up. Mine was about a foot long, the wavy patterns of gray steel marking the blade's quality. The walrus tusk handle had been my foster mother's contribution. It was no legendary sword, but it was a familiar weapon with a good grip and a good blade.

"Young man, come with me," the witch teased. "It will be so much better for you."

"I think I prefer the hospitality here," I called out, hoping it would be a true statement.

"But no one is home! No hospitality for you here. Come with me! I will show you things you have never seen before." Her voice was sweet as honey.

I looked right. Nothing there, just the house, which was more like a hall, stretching into the fog. I looked left and saw more of the house and a small clearing where the fog was less dense. I banged on the door with the butt of my seax, asking for hospitality without turning around.

"*Things like your insides,*" she continued, her voice now like a dull saw drawn over an old log.

I dared not show it, but the turning of her voice twisted my guts in ways I had never felt before. My seax nearly slipped from my hand as the nausea built up inside me. Even without meeting her gaze, this was a powerful enemy to deal with.

I thought about the sword in my pack, but dismissed it. Time spent unwrapping it would give her an opportunity to attack. Besides, I was not well enough practiced with a sword to wield one with any skill. The seax I at least knew how to wield with some minimum of competence. Could I get close enough to use it before being cursed? It might come to that, but better to avoid finding out.

The only choices were to stay by the door and hope someone answered or to move to where I could see more. I tried opening the door myself, but it was barred from the inside. Someone had to be there, I reasoned, so I stood my ground and banged again, promising stories and poetry.

The witch laughed at that. "What poetry do you know, pretty little man?"

I was not in the mood for composing and had little I could think of. There was one stanza that came to mind, though, if only to conjure an idea of what I might hope for.

"Roof-rider," I said, hoping that term would get her attention, "I know *all* the poetry." Those might have been my last words, but at least I would die bravely quoting Odin himself as he boasted about magic he knew:

> "I know a spell;
>   if I spy witches
> playing up in the air;
> I can loose this spell
>   so that they get lost,
> so they fail to find their skins,

so they fail to find their
minds."

"OH, PRETTY MAN . . ." said the witch, snorting as she laughed. The air became very quiet then. Not a sound of animals or wind.

I clutched my seax and swiveled my head from front to right, right to front. Left, every other time, just to be certain. I was as ready as I might be, I thought.

She came from above.

I cursed myself for not anticipating that, my only saving grace that I heard her cloak flutter above me before I saw her. I dove forward, tumbling over my outstretched hand, but dropped my seax in the process.

She slammed down like an iron-nosed bird of prey and cratered the ground upon which I had just stood. Her cloak, doubtless a thing of some power, spread out and then folded around her like a bat's wings. I scrambled away, toward the more visible area at the front of the house.

"Odin knows such a spell," she said, turning toward me, "but Odin does not share knowledge. So unless you hung for nine nights on a windswept tree, I think you know not—"

A thick piece of firewood flew out of the fog, its aim uncanny, its velocity shocking. It struck her in the face so hard she dropped her distaff and fell straight on her ass. Hands to her face could not stem the torrent of blood flowing through her fingers as she stood back up. The wet crunch of what was formerly her nose and the ensuing shriek of surprise and pain rang in my ears. I stepped back to steady myself.

"Now we all know such a spell," said a man leaning on a stick. He reached for another piece of firewood with a casual air quite at odds with how hard he might throw it. His wide-brimmed hat covered his face but for a wry grin and a bright silver beard.

The witch's nasal hiss did little to help her regain her threatening posture. She ran a few steps, making an awkward, bubbly noise, trying to sound dangerous and failing. Realizing she had forgotten her distaff, she paused, ran back, and picked it up.

"Are you afraid to meet my gaze, lady?" said the old man.

So challenged, she could not resist. Up went her glare in open hostility against the man. I chanced a look at her face then, since she was not looking at me. The prettiness I had assumed from my first attempt to see her was there, her features not too soft, not too sharp. Except for her eyes. Around her eyes, black veins shot out in every direction as if filled with poison. Those were not her eyes, but the eyes of a spirit she must have bound to aid her. I was glad to not have met them with my own gaze, and wondered at the fate of this man for having done so.

He did not sound like his limbs had been locked, however.

"By his looks, my friend has had a difficult journey. Perhaps you would leave your cloak for him? That would be most appropriate, I think."

I saw hate in the witch's bloodied face. Hate and power from a deep well of lore few would dare to learn. If she had indeed called a spirit and held it captive, it fled the old man's stare.

The veins thinned and receded. Her snarl dropped as her eyes widened while the rest of her skin went three shades paler. Fear had dawned on that venomous face. She flung the cloak down and ran into the mist without another word.

The old man's laughter chased her through the mist like a pack of hungry wolves.

It would have been funny if not for the context. I had just escaped one threat, and now I found myself alone with something that had caused that threat to flee in terror.

THE SORCERER'S HOSPITALITY

THE MAN WITH THE GOOD THROWING ARM was so inconspicuous as to make the lack of notable details the most notable detail about him. He stopped leaning on his walking stick and held it over one shoulder. His cloak was neither shabby brown nor a vibrant color that would indicate enough money for good dyes. Gray. Everything was a shade of gray, including his broad-brimmed hat, other than the bright silver sheen to his long but well-groomed beard.

"I'm not going to touch that thing," I said, nodding toward the cloak. "It was dyed in blood."

"A wise choice," replied the man. "I only meant to deprive her of it. I've seen ill things come from such objects in my travels."

"Lucky your travels took you here. You really know how to throw your wood around. But how did you find this house in the fog? I only managed by a raven's advice."

"The best spells are often the simplest ones. And it is my house, so I would hope I would not lose it."

"The door is barred from the inside."

"Is it?" He dropped the firewood and strode forward. His was a confident gait, that of a man unconcerned about his safety. I tried to mirror that confidence in picking up my seax, because nothing was worse than showing fear or indecision.

He ignored me. His stick was the only weapon I could see. Whatever weapon he held at his waist, and I knew there had to be at least one, was concealed by his cloak. Maybe he kept a sword or axe there. Or just more firewood to throw at people.

His back to me, he fumbled with the latch such that I could not see him do it. A moment later he stepped away from the open door, beckoning me in.

Could I have missed something as I tried to open the door? I did not think so. There was more to the man and more to the house than either let on. I just didn't know what.

"You are far from home I think," he said, "but you are safe in this place. I am a simple farmer here. My name is Hrani. Welcome."

We both knew his name was a lie. It was not his first and would not be his last. 'Simple' was also lie, for he had a strange way of speaking that I could not put down to one place. I knew many more languages than West and East Norse, but I could not place his accent. Nor could I think of a reason a 'simple' man would settle in such a place. More than that, his manner was far too confident for some bumpkin living in the woods. All of which led me to wonder how 'safe' I was.

"Farmer, eh?" I said. "And what do you farm here, in this house built for a jarl?"

If that seemed unnecessarily impudent, just consider two things: one, I am unnecessarily impudent by nature, which is probably why I learned to run, ski, climb, and swim faster and farther than anyone I knew; and two, Hrani had already told me two lies before he got to his supposed name. 'Farmer' was almost laughable.

Now that I had time to observe and not just fight for my life, the quality of the structure struck me. It was entirely out of place. The house was not dug into the earth. It was built straight up from the level ground, an expensive proposition in time and materials. Not the doing of just one man, and not for just one man. This was a place to host guests, or it was of little use.

"You look like you come from good stock," said Hrani. "What is your name?"

"I did not realize I looked like a cow," I replied. "Is that what you keep around in this forest? A bunch of cows?"

"Hmmm!" said Hrani, glaring at me sidelong, his lips still turned up in an unbroken smile.

"Because that is where I hear cows like it best," I said. "In the forest, where they can eat tree bark. Or maybe you cut out the complexities of such farming and just harvest the tree bark. Is that the kind of farming you do, Hrani?"

"You want to begin a battle of wits, but without even introducing yourself," said Hrani. "How out of order! I like it." He paused then to scratch at the mud with his stick. He looked at the sky and added, "The gloaming is upon us. I regret that I only offer hospitality to men I know." He turned his sidelong glance away and headed into the house.

My mind conjured a flash of yellow and red eyes staring at me through the darkness. The light would fade soon. If I took any longer, I was certain my imagination could conjure something even more terrifying than glowing eyes. And if the raven spoke true, my imagination had a very good idea of what was out there, just beyond the fog. I made my choice in less than a second.

"Ansgar Styrgrimsson."

Hrani stopped, facing fully away from me. He turned his head to ask his next question. "Styrgrimsson . . . You mean Styrgrim the Dangler is your father?"

"No, he was from Rogaland. He died last year. A raid went poorly, and his own men hanged him."

"His luck was overstretched, it seems. Styrgrim Church-Nose then?"

"Not him either. He took passage on a ship headed for Rome last year."

"For raiding, I hope," said Hrani, stroking his beard. "Though I doubt it. You don't mean Styrgrim the famous warrior, by any chance? What was he called?"

I sighed. "If you mean Styrgrim the Bear," I said,

wishing not to speak on the topic, "who fought for Arrow-Odd, then yes."

Hrani turned towards me, eyes burning in the shadow of his house. "You know the whereabouts of many men—what about him?"

I took a deep breath and forced my fists to unclench. Hrani knew more than he let on, and I still could not see how that was. But whatever his angle, I needed shelter for the night, and so further rudeness was perhaps not in order despite the man's suspicious personage. "Riches in Miklagard is what he was headed for, so he said," I answered. "That was nearly two years ago. There has been no word since."

Hrani opened his arms in welcome. It was as if he had just verified my story rather than heard it for the first time. "Welcome, son of Styrgrim," he said, gesturing me to follow him through the door.

I hesitated at the entrance, my head swiveling left and right, and I considered taking my chances out on my own under the moon. The fog had grown thicker by the minute in that low-lying place, and I still could not see how far the building extended. Nor could I see much in the other direction or behind me. That left no direction but forward despite my suspicion. It would be a foolish choice either way, but I at least smelled a savory stew of root vegetables and herbs inside.

That was enough to propel me forward. What can I say? I have a weakness for good food, even if I need to wander into a trap to eat it.

The house was a great hall on the inside,

stretching back an impossibly long way. A dozen torches at least lit the hall on each side, illuminating the painted shields hung between them. Each was a different coloration and depiction. All the designs on the shields were animals of different sorts. A falcon, a salmon, a ram, a boar—two different boar designs actually—and more. Ornate carvings crept up the support pillars. Animal heads connected to woven tendrils all along the supports, and these wrapped around runes carved into the wood.

This was old wood—very old. Some of the runes were worn down so that they were difficult to read. It was not clear what they meant in any case. These were the old runes, the kind only used for magic anymore rather than for carving messages.

Benches were set lengthwise down the hall, a hearth fire between every pair. If the man needed to feed an army, he could do so here, though no servants to maintain all these fires showed themselves. Right now, the benches were empty save for the chainmail running along those seats.

Only a rich jarl might own such a place, and I knew some whose halls were not so grand. This house belonged in the middle of a thriving port city, not hidden in a forest. The hall spoke of a man who was half-warrior and half-sorcerer.

So a trap it seemed, although a comfortable trap judging from the aromas of food and the warmth of the fire. And perhaps a trap I could talk my way out of. Skalds are good at that, and I was a good skald. If Hrani was a sorcerer, and I was pretty sure he was, that was fine. Sorcerers may be dangerous, but they can never resist battles of wit. If he was a god in disguise, well, the stakes were higher, but the same logic applied.

I sat down at Hrani's wordless gesture while he fetched food and drink.

"This is no backwoods structure," I told my host.

"And I offer no backwoods hospitality," he said as he laid down a steaming bowl of stew and handed me a horn full of mead. "You are suspicious I am more than a farmer. It is true that I have a good deal of lore I can call up when I have need of it."

That was a long-winded way of saying "I'm a sorcerer." And about as straightforward as I would expect.

Hrani didn't join me for food, but took a horn for himself before sitting down. His tone became more soothing as our conversation went on. Every question I posed had an answer, and every hint of untowardness was laughed off. All my questions were answered with questions themselves.

How are you so rich to build this house and serve mead? *Haha! What is a house but wood of the forest? What is mead but honey and the patience to let it sit for a while?* How are you kept safe with danger around? *Haha! How would those fools find this place in such heavy fog?*

My life, at least, should be safe. A sorcerer would hold to a promise of hospitality. Breaking such a promise could have dire consequences for him. Still, I could not shed my suspicion he was dangerous. If not to my life, then to what?

I finished my stew and downed the horn of mead. Refilling for both of us, Hrani started in on his own inquiries. They began generally enough on my family background. How I was fostered by my grandparents and saw my father little. What did I know of my father's exploits, and oh, my mother died of illness when I was very young? How interesting.

The sound of Hrani's voice became higher and sweeter as he asked questions that made me cringe. I had no good defense against them, unlike Hrani, who had a backstory prepared and was practiced in explaining away any inconsistent details about himself. With no way to deflect, I became less confident. And with less confidence often comes greater belligerence.

"You must need a guide to deal with the Swedes," said Hrani, draining his horn and rising to fill it again. "They can be most unintelligible at times."

"I won't have such trouble," I said, my blood suddenly up at the implied insult. "Anyone can understand East Norse, even when the Swedes garble it. Granted, they might play trickery by trying another tongue, but to little benefit. Sami I know, to speak to those neighbors of the Norse and Finns. Frankish as well, despite the Franks keeping clear of the Danes. Latin and Greek are familiar to me. You won't find many in the north who know those languages." That would tell him!

"Oh, but how well do you know any of them?"

asked Hrani with a dismissive shrug. "Well enough to change money, perhaps."

"Well enough, old man!" I was standing and shouting now, angry out of all proportion. "Well enough to tell great stories from the north in one language and all!" Hrani had poked at my pride just a little bit, my senses softened with mead and insecurity. "Would you like to hear one?"

"Yes." The answer came slithering out like a forked tongue. "But not just any story. Tell me something I have not heard. Tell me something I don't yet *know*. Tell me of Odin's altruism or Thor's thought-savvy, Frey's fidelity or Loki's loyalty."

He thought he had me there. Those were the opposites of how each god was known. Hrani had made a mistake, however. Stories of the gods were told differently by different people, and sometimes the variation was huge. One such story involved Thor dealing with a dwarf that had come to marry one of his daughters. I had made the mistake of telling my foster father Thor was dumb and lucky, but Halstein set me straight. In our village, we valued patience and a little vulgar humor as important parts of wisdom.

"That is quite the request," I said. "Why so specific, Hrani? Have you never heard of the wisdom of Thor?"

"O-ho!" Hrani cheered and stood up, his eyes wide with excitement. "What a salty skald you are! Of the four things I mentioned, you choose the least likely? You are either a fool or a *drengr* to face a challenge so boldly. I will be impressed if you can do it, but shall we make a wager? Your sword to be delivered, perhaps."

There was no 'perhaps' in his tone, and it made my blood rise even further until all I could see was battle. I rose to take Hrani's bait, failing to see how he had built it slowly. "What do you have to wager against that is as valuable?" I demanded. "And can I carry it?"

"It is something you already have but can easily take with you. I will give you my help. Don't laugh! You were happy to have it when that witch was upon you. Either way, I will escort you out of this forest, but if you win, I will share in some of the lore I know. A new thing wagered against a new thing."

And so I began by telling the story of Alviss the All-Wise:

Alviss is a dwarf who knows a lot of lore. While Thor is away, Alviss secures a promise to marry one of the hammer god's daughters. When Alviss shows up to collect her, Thor has returned, and that is where things get interesting.

Thor introduces himself and demands Alviss answer his questions before allowing his daughter to marry. Questions about what elves, men, gods, and *jǫtnar* call all manner of things, testing the dwarf's wisdom. Alviss answers them all!

But some dwarves are more sensitive than others, and Alviss is the sun-sensitive kind. By the time Thor is done asking questions, the sun rises and turns wise old Alviss to stone.

"I know this story," said Hrani, yawning. "It is no

great thing. A half-wit could have taken instruction to ask questions as well as Thor did."

"Oh, but that is where you are wrong," I countered. "You think Thor won with his questions, but he won before he ever asked any. He won at the beginning when he introduced himself."

A single eyebrow from Hrani shot up so high I thought it would take the roof off. "'I am Thor' is all he says. What of that granted him victory?"

"In Rogaland they tell the tale that way, the blandest telling possible. In Halogaland it is 'I am Hammer-Thor,' because of course they do. But in Sygnafylki, or at least my village Dafvik, we tell it differently. There it is 'I am Horse-Dick Thor!'"

"Ha!" said Hrani, shaking his head. "I think you have failed to show any wisdom with that example. Perhaps you would care to try another."

I ignored the old man and continued.

"'I am Horse-Dick Thor,' he says, daring the dwarf to continue his challenge. So ensues a battle of wits: Alviss the dwarf, the All-Wise, rises to answer each question with the grandest poetry. What names does he know, and who uses them? Wind-weaver is the sky, and whirling-ball the moon, though these aren't the only names for either one. Wood is called nothing more than fuel by *jǫtnar*, mane of the plains by the gods, to name a few favorites.

"Alviss, seeking to impress, continues answering questions without considering when they will end. One must imagine the dwarf rather impressed with himself—answering questions the asker is not likely to know in the first place. At least he will depart leaving the ignoramus with some more knowledge than he had before! After all, the crude Horse-Dick Thor could use a little culture.

"So on the dwarf droned, more pleased with himself the closer he got to his doom. Horse-Dick Thor could not possibly know any better than to keep asking questions, he must have surmised. And that is why Thor won at the beginning, not the end: in his introduction, he created an expectation in the dwarf, which kept Alviss from seeing the danger he was in. Only then could Thor ask questions over and over until the sun came up.

"And so, unpretentious, unsophisticated Thor let no laugh escape him when the dwarf named the sun 'Dvalin's plaything.' He let the reference slide. In our version, Thor later speaks to the stone Alviss and says a name for the sun was missed in all those references: 'Wit's end.'"

Hrani was covering his mouth by this time and staring into the hearth fire. Soon he could not contain his smile anymore and laughed out loud. It was a brutal thing that could have doubled as a war cry as much as a chuckle, but I knew it meant I had won.

"Well, skald, that was indeed impressive. Though some might claim it is the wisdom of Dafvik more than the wisdom of Thor on display."

"Let them claim," I said. "It is only a story in any case."

"Only a story! And this from a skald! Nothing could be less true. I will pay you in kind for your story, however. You told me something new, and I will give you the same. You know the Words of the High One? I heard you speak some to that witch."

Words of the High One. The *Hávamál*. Now there was a poem with no standard telling. Variants were so wide you might swear the people in the valley next to yours were foreigners for how little the two versions might overlap.

"I know it," I said. "At least ten versions of it. What of it?"

"And in all those versions, how many tell you that cattle die and kinsmen die, but that word-fame lives on?"

"That is a common thread in all I have heard."

"And what weaves that thread through all those different tellings, do you think? Stories are never just stories. They are the vessels of the dead, for good or ill. They breathe life into history, give form to wisdom. Spirits ride those stories still, and what are their alternatives? To disappear. Or to linger unattached to memory or word-fame, a hateful existence."

"What do you mean, 'to linger unattached to memory?'"

"I mean to return after death and haunt the living!"

"*Draugar*, you mean."

Miserable people who died might not remain dead. Or rather, they did remain dead, the problem being that they were still walking around at night attacking livestock or people. Lucky for all of us, their roaming range was generally very small, if they even left their barrows at all.

"Yes, and if you understood the importance of your stories, you would know how to deal with them."

"I have no dealings with them at all. They are not difficult to avoid."

"Ah, you haven't so far. But in case you must, here is where I return wisdom for wisdom by telling you how to deal with such things. You will not over-power them, as they are strong. You will not kill them, as they are already dead. Maybe you can de-stroy those still-moving corpses, but it will take fire or dismemberment. Their weakness, however, will be their misery in life. Over-attached to some object or idea, something they cannot let go of to move on. Something of their vanity or wealth."

"So the dwarf Fafnir, why did he become a dragon and not a *draugr*?"

"Because he was not dead! He was alive, if you can call it that, and cared only for his hoard of gold. It turned him into a hideous thing because of his at-tachment. Just as the same attachment calls to a foolish man's mind and never lets go. Look for that if you encounter the malignant dead, and destroy it. Sever the connection before the dead man eats your face."

Advice to live by.

I could not deny the quality of Hrani's lore. He was right about Fafnir letting all that gold turn him into a slithering dragon. So too could a man too attached to his money or land return to it. *Draugar* were rare and haunted only small spaces where they were known. To be avoided at nearly any cost—they could tear down houses with their hands and curse you for the rest of your life. If the old man was right, this was their one weakness. Assuming you knew what they were attached to from life.

I decided to pass that wisdom on the first chance I had. As for actually testing it, that would be for more heroic men. If I saw Judgment again, I was certain he would be willing to trade for the wisdom I had won. My battle of wits with a sorcerer was its own story, even more to trade should I have the need.

I would need that and much more in short order.

CHAPTER 4

THE FARMER'S TASK

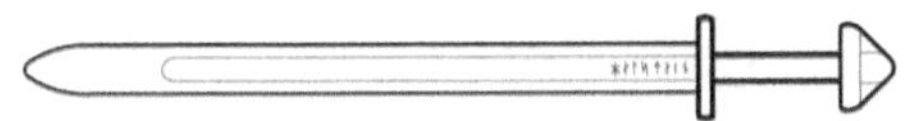

THE LAST THING I RECALLED WHEN I AWOKE the next day was drowsily sipping mead and feeling even more smug than usual. It is part of the magic inherent to alcohol to make one more foolish while at the same time making one feel wiser. It would be a while before I realized such magic applied to me as much as the next man. At that time, I was almost as stupid about drinking as I was about women.

I bid Hrani good morning, and he offered a loaf of coarse bread. It was about all I could stomach, the lingering smell of stew not nearly so pleasant in that context as it had been the night before. I was still sus-picious of the old man, but did not feel he was a threat. Besides, he had given good hospitality and promised to lead me out of the forest.

We soon left the hall and walked in silence through the woods. The paths were many, but the old man knew the right ones to take. The trees were dense and let in little light, but at least there was no fog. We cleared a final treeline as the hills began a gentle up-slope into wide grassy areas, and he bade me head due south from there to find the farm I sought.

I turned around, intending to ask him his real name, the courage of finality swelling up in me. He was already gone.

I counted myself lucky for his hospitality and lucky a second time for our parting. Sorcerer, yes, but that could mean a lot of things. Too much truth can overwhelm a man, even a skald. Had he been a prophecy-man, I might have been bound to hear my future. And in no story I have ever heard has that turned out well for the one hearing his prophecy.

Hrani might also have been a god in disguise, as you never know when that cheeky lot is going to give you a line and a false smile just to see how you react. But I couldn't pin him down on one in particular. Odin, maybe, though I would have expected Odin to have only one eye.

In any case, it is better to be forgotten by the gods. Too much attention from them is usually bad luck, so I did not lament his disappearance too much.

Soon the path opened to a green meadow, as inviting as the forest had felt dangerous. The morning sunlight was most welcome, not just to warm me but to help guide my direction. Then I hit a thick canopy of trees again and I had to trust my senses to stay on a southward track. These forests were no less dense and just as cold but seemed to open up at my feet and allow easy passage.

The *landvættir* approved, obviously, despite remaining unseen. I had never encountered such a spirit of the land that I knew of, but I could often feel their presence. A gust of wind to cool my hot forehead, a peek of light through the branches to show me where the sun was—these were not chance happenings.

So I made good time until I happened upon a goatherd clad in a heavy brown cloak. He was nestled under a spruce tree, eyeing a few goats out in the bright sun. The lowest branches by the ground were cut away just enough to enshroud a man-sized shape, maybe even protect him from the weather. A large man, no question, but still a man. He was not doing much herding, not that I blamed him for seeking out a comfortable place in the shade, especially in case of the weather turning.

My foster father had sent me to herd sheep once when I was thirteen, and the boredom snared me from the very first hour of my watch. My wandering mind did not do well with that task. When I came out of my inevitable daydreaming, there was one ewe left in sight. It took me three days to find the rest, two of those days in the driving rain.

"Good afternoon," I said.

"Mrmmph," came the response. The muffled voice was low and gravelly. A hood covered the man's nodding head, and a rat-eaten cloak covered him all the way to his feet. A long wooden staff laid across his body was the only other distinguishing feature visible.

Goatherds are not the brilliant reciters of stories and gossip that ravens are. They are, however, reliable with their directions. Better than ravens, goatherds will often tell what they know for the pleasure of a conversation. I didn't need eyeballs to trade or even a story to come up with. I had, however, hoped for more of a response than 'Mrmmph.'

"Um, are you a goatherd?" I asked and immediately wished I had not. A rotten smell wafted down at the same time. "I just saw your staff and the goats nearby and assumed, well—it seemed the logical conclusion. I know a little about herding myself. But . . ." *But if you're a half-wit I will leave you alone, especially if that is you I smell.* "But I will not distract you. I am only on my way to find Folki's farm."

Again the long and heavy nod.

I looked away, in part because I hoped for something else to distract me from conversation with the half-wit. Smoke hung low over the trees in the distance, only a few miles away, and that was more than enough. If it was not Folki's farm, the inhabitants would know where it was.

"It seems to be that way, by the smoke," I said. "Good day to you."

I took my cue to take my leave, thanked the half-witted goatherd, and strode off. The goats showed more interest than their warden and bleated softly as I passed. Hungry things and more skittish than I knew most goats to be. Goats had their place, and that place was simmering in a stew. Stew! My appetite had returned, and I imagined what a relief it would be if I could reach Folki's farm that same night.

Folki was a rich man, or else I would not be delivering such an expensive weapon to him. That meant good meat and ale for sure. That thought in mind, I redoubled my pace as thoughts of food and drink and sleeping under a roof drew me onward. Two hot meals in two nights would be great luck indeed.

It was a long walk, but the sight of my objective made my feet all the lighter. It was after dark when I knocked on the door. Too late for most guests, but if I had the right farm, I was expected. Still, it was reasonable that Folki would treat any person as suspicious until shown otherwise. I moved away from the door and sat on the woodpile nearby to give time and space for a response.

The house was short and squat, with moss growing on the roof. The lumber they had used to build it was thick, and the structure gave the impression of being old but sturdy and reliable. No longhouse like Hrani's magical dwelling, this was a farmhouse where both the people and animals would stay warm in the winter months.

Folki sure took his time. Minutes went by, and I began to wonder what was going on. No way could my knocking have gone unheard, even had everyone been asleep. A thrall would have heard it and woken the man. Should I knock again? Would that be rude?

It was one thing to be rude to crazy sorcerers camped out in the middle of the forest—they probably didn't know much other than rude behavior.

But this was a man of means and wealth, controlling a large farm, or series of farms, depending on how you defined his holdings.

I did not want to be rude by knocking too aggressively, but did not wish to depart without a word. It would take me at least a day to find his nearest neighbor, I was sure, and that was assuming I knew what direction to walk in. So should I knock again or continue waiting?

Niceties of this sort were the kind that made me question my sanity. Witches and wargs in the forest, *draugar* holed up in their mounds, all those had some reason or logic to them. But manners in the north? That was something I had to tread carefully with, because what seemed like a straight path rarely ever was.

In the middle of all this self-doubt, the flat of a spearhead fell heavy onto my shoulder. An uncommon way to say 'Hello,' though not unheard of.

"Hello," I answered, only with words.

"It is a late hour for a man to seek hospitality," said a woman's voice.

"It might just be very early if I was otherwise to arrive in the morning," I said, wondering who was holding the spear. "The route from Dafvik is not an easy one, but I made good time. If this is not Folki's house, I can be on my way. Perhaps I can take my chances with a goatherd's hospitality instead."

Silence. That would give her something to think about—the implied accusation that she, whoever she was, would be stingy with room and board, was not a challenge she could ignore. To potentially be shown up by a goatherd! It was unthinkable. Still, whoever this woman was would have to acquiesce only under protest to avoid seeming too eager. Welcome to the niceties of living in the north.

The flat of that spearhead leapt up to kiss my cheek. Not hard, not soft.

"It is his house by definition," she said. "Welcome."

I rose from my seat on the woodpile and turned, the weapon retreating to its owner's shoulder. "You've handled a spear before," I said. This was an uncommon woman. Most would remain indoors for their work. This one was ready, maybe even eager, to defend her home with more than the cooking or weaving tools that had doubtless been foisted upon her.

Helmed and clad in a mail shirt, she showed her teeth with a wolfish smirk. "There is roast pig inside. I stuck and bled him myself. He will not be the last." She turned and went inside, golden braid swinging behind her, and I was left wondering if that had been an invitation or a threat. Probably both. Violence was the way of humor for most people I knew, or at least when they had a sense of humor. If nobody was bleeding, what was there to laugh about?

Better to avoid further insinuation on my part, then. Besides, I was hungry.

I followed in slowly, waiting a few beats and then walking in and taking my time shutting the door behind me. It would give anyone plenty of opportunity to see I was no threat.

Four thralls stood about with knives in hand and eyed me as I entered. They did not look hungry. They looked afraid. And fearful people holding knives tended to be dangerous.

"Was I not invited in?" I asked. I had taken the woman's appearance for granted, but there was real fear in the eyes upon me. "This house appears prepared for an attack. I regret I am a humble delivery man offering no such violence."

My eyes ran to the middle of the main room, where half a piglet hung above dim embers. The aromas of smoke and roasted pig flesh brought me back to feasts held at home when my foster mother would stuff an animal with salt and secret herbs. Her machinations made meat into meals no one would forget. This was simpler than her doing, but I could still taste the dripping fat even as I saw it. The skin had crisped up and would crunch better than dry bread crusts.

"Other than to raid your larder, perhaps," I said, licking my lips.

"Watch out," said the oldest of the thralls. Or so I sized her up, based on manner and clothing. She held a long seax straight out in front of her, standing farther forward than the other, younger thralls. "Invited in, but who is—the skin I see or a rider? Are they the same, or is it a lie?"

Fear shook her outstretched arm—one clearly not practiced at fighting, or else she would have kept her elbow bent. I was shit at fighting, and even I knew that. This posture meant she wanted me kept at bay.

She feared me but still faced me, so this was a thrall with courage.

"I am no skin-rider or roof-rider or rider of any kind," I said. "I am no sorcerer. Were you expecting a man to arrive with a spirit in him not his own?"

"We did not know what to expect when you knocked," said a voice from behind the thralls.

A man emerged from between them and placed a hand on the shoulder of the old thrall. Hair hung loosely about his face before he swept it up and behind in one wide-eyed motion, tired but trying to keep alert. His other hand revealed an axe that contrasted with his loose nightclothes, not even a belt on. Put that down to drowsiness, perhaps, since even I knew fighting in loose clothing was a bad idea.

"But my sister says you are no threat. You said you were delivering something?" He must have believed it, because he put his axe down.

"If you are Folki, I have something of yours."

A sword was a costly thing both in material and labor. Iron was not difficult to find, but making good steel out of it was no simple thing, much less that much good steel at once—it was not something common folk could afford. Fewer still could afford the work of my foster father.

"Yes, of course. I am Folki. My sister Aud greeted you already. I did not think you would be here so soon, but it is good that you are! I am in need of such a weapon, or you would have met with a friendlier welcome straight away. It is good to have a skald in the house, even aside from the sword."

It must be a fine thing to be so wealthy you can buy wares from Halstein the Smith and then forget you had spent the money.

Unlatching my pack let loose a tension of days I had taken for granted. Wrapped three times over, not including its scabbard, the weapon was tucked away tightly, bound to my pack so it would not hang loose and flap against me. It felt good to take off the weight. "Here, see? I am no liar," I said. The wrappings fell away as if they had been tight bandages protecting an injured limb, and soon pommel and hilt glinted in the firelight.

"I can tell you he is no liar," said Aud, now unhelmeted. "He does not have the eyes for it."

"What kind of eyes does he have then?" said the thrall.

"Hungry. Ragna, pour the man a drink. My brother can examine his sword without assistance, I think."

Finally, a bit of hospitality. The mood was a cheerier one. The thralls eased away, showing less inclination to stab me. Ragna, now no longer concerned I was a witch riding someone else's skin, retrieved a horn of suitable size and filled it. I passed the sword on to its new owner and accepted the drink at the same moment—a fair trade.

"And plenty more," croaked Ragna, giddy with amusement. "That will keep the goats safe! A skald is a sign of good luck. Drink and drink and drink!" She hiked back the sleeve of her shirt, revealing arms with a sun-worn look, as she busied herself clearing a spot near the fire. This woman had done hard work outside for much of her life. She was one tough old lady, if a bit addled, or I was no judge of anything.

The accurate thing to tell you was I took that horn straight over to the roasting pig and started ripping off pieces of meat with one hand while I downed ale with the other. But you don't need a description of me eating. You want to know about the sword, and why not? Folki paid quite a sum for it upfront, and I carried it for a week to make certain he received it in good time. So while I stood munching and gulping, Folki unsheathed it to have a look.

Men can never resist doing this. Hand one a sword, he's going to take it out of the scabbard and look it up and down. The ignorant ones will touch the cutting edge, but that's a bad idea. Grime from fingers is bad for a blade, so those who know what they're doing look but don't touch, or at least know to clean and oil the blade immediately.

"It's magnificent!" he said.

Waves and pools of gray on gray showed the nature of its craftsmanship. Not the bright, gleaming show-blades of cheap steel trying to compensate in looks for what they lacked in sharpness. This had the keen understatement of steel ingots twisted and hammered and folded over and over and over. That was what Halstein did, perhaps better than anyone in the western fjord lands, and why rich men were willing to pay a premium for his wares.

Even if those rich men had not enough sense to

keep their fingers off the fuller. From the corner of my eye, I could tell Folki was a toucher.

"You will cut yourself doing that," said Aud.

"I am not so careless as you say, sister," said Folki, which he followed with a hissed inhalation. He withdrew his thumb and pretended not to notice the blood blooming upon it. "Hjalti left the farm under my care, and care I will take of it. Skald! This weapon is the thing I needed, but I could still use some assistance. You are welcome here for the night, but I say stay tomorrow and come with me. It will earn you glory and gold and perhaps a good new story."

So Folki was ready for a fight, at least according to him. So ready that he needed an object lesson to remind him swords were sharp. I filled my mouth with too much pork to be able to answer anytime soon and chewed all the slower to give me time to think. And I thought: *No, that is probably a terrible idea, whatever the details are.* The details were probably along the lines of *I heard of a powerful sorcerer in the forest, so I'm going to find him and whip out my sword and wave it around until he tells me secrets.*

"Who is Hjalti?" I asked, intending to delay and find an honorable reason to say no.

"Our brother. He went off raiding," said Aud.

"Oh, stop holding back details!" said Folki. "He signed on with Styrgrim and sailed for who knows where. And will we ever see either one again?" He looked at me looking at him and perhaps thought better of the rhetorical nature of his question. "Safe travels to them, of course, but it has been some time now with no word. And so it falls to me to rid us of that menace."

"I could—" said Aud, before her brother cut her off.

"You are a woman! Mail shirt and helm do not make a warrior."

"And a sword flopping in a limp wrist does?"

Never get involved in family arguments. In fact, try not to get involved in any arguments, but especially not the family kind. No good can come from it, just as I suspected no good would come from joining Folki's errand.

"The journey from Dafvik was long," I said. "And more treacherous than I expected. I prefer to take the long route back rather than retrace my steps, so I should leave sooner rather than later. Tell me of this menace, and I can tell it as a story on my way back. It might recruit you a few good fighters."

"Hjalti could have protected the goats," murmured Ragna in a mournful tone.

"The goats are hardly the point," snapped Folki. He shook his head as if to shake off any more talk of goats. "The point is, we cannot go out at night. Fewer and fewer go out even in the day for fear of the dead. I killed a man in my employ soon after Hjalti left, and now he stalks the farm. One of my friends was killed after visiting here, another we found who was expected but never arrived. Now, none of our neighbors come to visit or trade."

"A *draugr*?" I said. "They usually stay in their barrows if you leave them alone and don't try to steal their hoards. Why this one would stalk your farm—wait, what was this man killed over?"

Folki set his jaw. Aud looked away, half embarrassed and half-amused.

Only Ragna was eager to speak. "He was bad to the goats," she said, near spitting the words *bad* and *goats*.

The four of us stared into empty space, our imaginations all working far harder and in more detail than any of us wanted.

"More ale," I said, louder than necessary. I held out my horn to Ragna, and she was only too happy to refill it. "Avoid him," I said after another draft.

"I intend to seek him out and put him down for good," said Folki. With his left hand on his hip, he examined the blade in his right. "Will you come with me?"

"Come with *us*," corrected Aud.

"That sounds like the opposite of avoiding him," I said. "There is no good to come from fighting a *draugr*. Better to let them burn themselves out, even if you have to move. Or hire an outlaw to do it, if you would hire anyone. I have had enough strange encounters for one trip. I won an argument with a raven and got away from a witch. The goatherd was benign enough, but I don't trust the sorcerer in the woods and would prefer to stay even farther away from all of them, as well as the things that might like to eat me."

Now there was one detail missed by both Folki and Aud that they would have taken as rather frightening if they hadn't been busy with each other's egos.

Ragna was listening, though, as thralls often do better than their lords. All the color drained from her face.

"Y– you said . . . the goatherd?"

The heads of both Folki and Aud whipped around at me, their argument forgotten.

"Yes," I said. "I passed him to the north by a few miles. The man you hired to replace the goat—" I paused, mind full of kennings, none of which I wanted to voice. "The replacement. Or so I assumed."

Now the reader has probably long since surmised where this was going, and just about any more description I give is only going to belabor the point we both know is about to rear its ugly head. Why was I, the character in this story, so much slower than you, the reader of it? I can only tell you the mind tends to avoid terrible conclusions whenever possible. I was only a young man at the time, with no hard edge developed to accept hard truths as they appeared.

Besides, my mind reasoned, it could not be so bad as I thought since I had encountered him in the daylight.

"There has been no replacement. What did this man look like?" asked Folki, who had gone a shade paler since last he spoke.

"I don't know," I said. Mind and mouth slowed down as I spoke the next words, "He was covered in a heavy cloak and hood and sat enclosed in the thick branches at a tree trunk."

Aud stood up and hefted her spear. "What kind of tree was it?"

"Spruce?" I said, not so uncertain as my tone indicated.

Folki's sword-bearing wrist flopped, his strength draining with his color. "We buried Brestir under the eaves of a spruce. A few miles north of here."

"But he had goats!" I protested. "There was a herd of goats all around!"

"Under his spell!" shouted Ragna. "That's what they are! Haven't seen the goats for months now—*he's* got them!" This was not all the old woman had to say, but her voice soon became a noisy blur in my ears as I reconsidered how close I had come to death. On she went, insisting on what Hjalti would do if he were here, that something must be done, that the goats must be saved, until a noise cut her short.

Something heavy thudded onto the roof, and only that silenced the old thrall. Up she looked, and in horror clutched at her face. In a moment, she rode her fear and drew the long seax from behind her back, holding it upward in the same elbow-locked posture she had used on me earlier.

The air seemed to leave the place as dust and bits of roof sod fell to the floor. Silence followed, louder than any chorus of shouts might have been. My own brain screamed in alarm, and I waited, uncertain what I was waiting for, but something—anything—to indicate the thing on the roof was benign. A bear banging on the walls that only sounded like it came from the roof. A branch blown by high winds, hitting the house. Or a large flock of birds all fallen out of the sky and hitting the roof with simultaneous precision.

The thralls whimpered while the rest of us held a collective breath. No noise on the roof followed the great, shuddering thud. No footsteps telling of doom or clawing at the ceiling to get in. I reached behind my back for my seax, careful to draw in silence, and breathed out. Stories had power, and this one had shrouded us all in a fear of the dark. Out of that lightless mold our minds had sculpted the monstrosity coming out of the night to haunt us. One of the moon's minions, a great power only because we imagined it to be.

That was what I was thinking when we all heard a goat give a short bleat. It was not on the roof—that would have been ridiculous. It was just outside the door. One goat voice became two, then three, and then more than I could count. The tribe had returned.

"Mrmmph," came a low moan from the roof.

We listened, frozen in place, for Brestir the *draugr* to make his next move. One of the goats scratched at the door, its hooves loud against the solid oak. The noises outside grew to a fever pitch, fraying the nerves of all inside. Would Brestir move on, unable to enter through the door unless invited, as Ragna had indicated?

I never did answer that question to any satisfaction. In the next instant, Brestir crashed straight through the roof and crushed Ragna under his bulk.

He was blue as Hel and swollen to the size of an aurochs, near bursting out of the loose woolen cloak about him. His mouth was set into a stupid, ghoulish grin that I got a full view of as he turned to face me. One eye was angled up towards the ceiling and the other down towards the floor, the average of the two angles honing in on me. Much of his upper lip was gone, exposing what yellow teeth and rotting gums remained beneath the wisps of what was left of his beard. I could see why this *draugr* was not the talking type.

Brestir shook his head as he rose from Ragna's broken body. This would have been an opportune time for Folki to cleave Brestir neck to shoulder, but I can't blame the man for being just as frozen in fear as I was.

Brestir did not stand unimpeded, however. Aud drove him backwards with her spear and a war cry like one of Odin's valkyries. For all the *draugr's* bloated size and strength, he was still taken aback at the timing and could not get his footing. Neither did Aud's spear find his heart, however. The *draugr* dropped backwards to send the spearhead sailing over his face, and kicked Aud in the side with both feet. I heard the crack of at least one bone breaking. The blow sent Aud flying back past where she had been standing moments before.

Her cry brought Folki out of his idleness, enough

to take Aud's lead. He attacked before Brestir could rise to his full height, which was at least a head above mine. It was a fair swipe he took with that sword for effort, but not a good one for technique. I would have done no better. Brestir stepped inside the attack and blocked it at Folki's wrist, knocking him to the floor with sheer brute strength. The sword clattered away, and Brestir stood over Folki's prone form. This was not a predatory thing for the *draugr*; this was personal.

I have mentioned I was no fighter—a runner, climber, swimmer, and general avoider only. Nonetheless, I kept my seax very, very sharp for the few times I might need to use it. So when I drove its point into Brestir's back, it bit all the way down to the hilt.

You can't stop a *draugr* that way, as I was soon reminded.

Brestir's elbow smashed into the side of my head and sent both me and the room spinning. As I staggered for my balance against the door, the *draugr* loomed large over Folki. There was no time for running now, and I was certain I saw the shape of my death.

A skald will improvise or die, and Aud would have been one great skald. With no weapon at hand and no time to prepare, she had gathered up her armor with both hands and charged a second time. As Brestir fixed eyes on his would-be victim on the ground, Aud brought the heavy chain shirt around in a wide circle and whipped it across the *draugr*'s face.

A weapon it was not, but it *was* about twenty-five pounds of steel in the form of thousands of tiny ringlets. The sheer force of it snapped the *draugr*'s head sideways and tore off more of his rotting face. He was big and tough, but even he staggered back at the blow.

Aud grimaced from exertion and pain. It was a bold attack, but she was worse off than the *draugr*, and the *draugr* knew it. Brestir caught his balance and smiled with only part of a lip. He would catch her gaze if he could. The dead can use power in eye contact, and it would be worse than a witch locking her limbs.

Folki rose then and hefted his axe with one hand, pulling his injured sister behind with the other. Brestir turned to the farmer who would be a warrior and held him there with a look. That was enough to make most men cower or crumble, and Folki was not made for battle any more than I was. This appeared to be the end of the fight, but the farmer had more warrior in him than expected.

Folki laughed.

No low chuckle. This was a great, abusive howl right into the *draugr*'s half-face. The kind that speaks of challenge and delight in battle despite certain death. Folki refused to look away even as Brestir's stare wormed its way into him.

The *draugr* muttered some curse through its rotting mouth, and still Folki refused to budge.

"I took your life, and my sister took your face," said Folki. "But it seems to me you'll be no less popular with the ladies in town now than when you lived." With a roar of delight, he rushed wide-eyed and struck at the thing's head with his axe while his sister found her spear.

The *draugr* retreated but slapped away each attack before it could land. It would not be defeated that way. What next, then, other than inevitable demise and having our faces eaten?

Ragna had something to say about that. The old woman had but a few gurgles to get my attention as she pointed to my left. The sword lay there, half-hidden amongst the shadows of low firelight. I picked it up and hefted it threateningly as the three of us surrounded the *draugr*. It would be a losing fight, but not an easy one for our enemy.

"The . . . goats . . ." gasped Ragna, and breathed her last.

Hrani's advice flashed through my mind. *Sever the connection.* Ragna knew what needed doing. Hrani had all but told me straightaway. Indeed, a skald lives by improvisation, and I knew this one would seem insane to my hosts, but it had to be done.

I turned and ran out the door.

"Mrmmph!" cried the *draugr* in too-late understanding as I shut the door behind me. The sounds of slashing blades finding blue, rotting flesh followed. More unintelligible cries accompanied the *draugr*'s stomping and flailing attacks. Neither sibling was whole, but they had found enough of the rhythm of battle to fight as more than the sum of two injured people.

There were six goats, not one of them skittish any longer. One with a black and white striped face bleated low as it turned itself sideways. Under Brestir's spell, maybe, but that spell could not make them consent. This one at least seemed to know what was coming and felt relief because of it.

I brought the sword down on the back of its neck, severing the head with one clean strike. The others made no move to leave. A second fell, and then a third and more until I had severed all six of the *draugr*'s connections to this world.

The shriek that followed was worse than any sound Brestir had yet made. In the next instant, he crashed through the door, taking out parts of the wall on both sides, and once again making the whole house shudder. I stared down my enemy, summoning what courage I had left. This would be the final stroke one way or another, I thought.

But I was wrong. There would be no final strike, at least not on my part. Aud's spear shot lightning-like out from the house and took Brestir in the back of the skull. Without his goats, the *draugr* was a spirit with a loose tether. He could not shrug off another wound with an unintelligible grunt. All that came out of his mouth was the tip of a spear. The yellow light of his eyes dulled, and a great and irreversible exhalation whispered his end. His body dropped and tumbled over itself like a slow landslide, falling face-first just a few feet outside my striking range.

I owed Aud a drink and two to whoever taught her how to throw a spear. But that was no happy woman who stumbled out the door, clutching her midsection. To her mind, I had just run from the fight.

But I am a lucky skald, and she let me explain before trying to run me through.

THE POET'S CALLING

"SO NOW YOU KNOW THE STORY," I SAID.

I kicked my legs out and stretched in my high seat. I don't usually stop to rest in trees, but a skald makes his way by improvising, and I had a fondness for birches. This tree was a great old trunk for the first fifteen feet or so. The steep angles of its primary branches at that point created a butt-sized nest for me to settle myself into. As sleeping rough went, this would be quite the luxury. The *landvættir* still favored me, it seemed.

Luckier still, Judgment the raven found me just before twilight, looking to trade story for story. I had headed west instead of north when I set out. It would be a longer road, and I could use advice on the paths best avoided.

"I will trade directions for that!" croaked the raven, happier and less . . . well, judgmental than I took him for at our previous meeting. "And more. But one question: you said nothing good could come of fighting a *draugr*. But something good did come of it!"

He was referring to the siblings fighting alongside each other and, as I told it, how Folki had to accept his sister's martial prowess while Aud now respected her brother for laughing in the face of certain death.

They had both gone back to exactly the same responsibilities they'd had before, only for different reasons.

What I did not mention was the aftermath in the days that followed. Judgment read me right as my face darkened with his comment.

"Did you forget about Ragna?" I asked, trying to pivot away from the real issue. We had won that fight, but images lingered in Folki's mind when the light was low. There was indeed nothing good that could come from fighting a *draugr*. That thing's stare had done lasting harm. Folki shrieked in his sleep about unseen horrors and kept up the fires for light rather than heat. In the dark, he was not himself, and this was not the first time I had heard of such symptoms. If the other stories were any indication, Folki's condition would not improve with time.

"The thrall? Oh! What about her?"

"She died."

"Is that all?"

"She used her last breaths fighting. The *draugr* killed her, but she denied him victory."

"She was a thrall," said Judgment. "Not that I care. I'm a raven. We don't organize ourselves into absurd classes like you hairy brutes love to do." Judgment was still his old self. Not that I could disagree with him. "You all obsess about such distinctions. You don't care for your thralls as you care for your freemen or your lords. So shouldn't you not care about a thrall's death?"

I looked out over a rolling hillscape of leaves. My tree was tall and situated upon a small hill over-looking thick forest to the north and west. Tree was piled upon tree so thick their tops looked like water rippling as a gentle wind made its way through them.

"I might also have been a thrall had my father not fostered me to his own parents. I don't value thralls so lightly. They often have good stories to tell—the kind you won't hear from more comfortable men. And I do care that she died. She was good-humored and tough and kind, and I lament not hearing any of her stories. We gave her a good funeral pyre. I lived one story alongside her. I won't ride her courage to victory just to forget it in the mud after. I'm no *níðingr.*" The force coming into my voice in those last sentences surprised even me.

"All right, all right!" said the bird. "I wasn't im-pugning you personally."

"Just all of humanity?"

"Maybe a little bit," he said without hesitation or irony, and we shared a laugh. "Speaking of im-pugning humanity, did you find that farmer I told you about?"

"Farmer! Some farmer you sent me to!" I said, shaking my head. I had not mentioned it, thinking the beginning of my story to trade would be meeting the goatherd who was not a goatherd. "That was a sorcerer! I was lucky to get away with my life."

"He had good mead, though."

"He did have good mead. Wait, did you meet him? And since when do ravens drink mead?"

"Ravens get up to all manner of things you might not expect," said Judgment. "And yes, I met him. You weren't listening to my warning about that witch sneaking up on you and I had to get out of there before she saw me too. But I thought I would circle a bit to check on you."

"You mean check to see if I was dead so you could eat my eyes?"

"Exactly. But I didn't find your delicious corpse. I only found a crazy old man who wouldn't give me his name, just said he was 'hooded one.' Like that would be intimidating and mysterious. He didn't have any stories to trade, just expected me to give up my information for a drink! I don't know about him being a sorcerer. I would have expected a sorcerer to be better at riddles."

"He gave his name as Hrani, not that I believe it. You got out with all your feathers, I see."

"By the skin of my beak!" said the raven, an octave higher than normal. He flapped his wings in excitement a few beats and then settled down. "You know what I mean. I didn't want to trade information for a drink, so he said he would trade wisdom. I'm for that, but then he started talking some bollocks about Thor and dwarves and penises. Can you believe that?"

"Perhaps he didn't tell it right," I said with a smile. "He was a sorcerer, after all, and not a skald."

"Well, I wasn't even listening once he started with the stupid names for everything. Like I care about that! I was so mad, I challenged him to a game of riddles. That fool agreed, so I went first and asked him, 'What do Odin's ravens say about him when the old man can't hear?' No answering that, and oh was he mad about it! Took a swipe at me with his stick as I flew off. I tried to shit on his head, but that wide-brimmed hat saved him from the worst of it. I stole a sip of mead on my way out! Maybe you should pay him another visit and tell him to treat his guests better."

I laughed a deep, throaty laugh. The kind of laugh you think you can stop, and you're replaying what was just said in your mind, and then it seems even funnier than the first time. I leaned back against the largest branch to avoid falling and shouted my joy to the sky. That was one of the funniest things I had ever heard, and I did not care who knew.

Mastering myself after a minute, I finally replied in all seriousness that I intended to avoid Hrani the Not Farmer if I could. "If he is still there, he may want something of me I do not care to give. And if he is not, everything else there may want to eat parts of me I do not want eaten."

I was grateful for the companionship, something I had not felt before from birds who were such strict deal-makers. The raven was good for his word as far as the directions were concerned. He told me of safe paths stretching far enough west for me to find the rest of the way on my own. It was a deep and restful sleep in the tree that night. The birch felt like a straw bed at the end of a hard journey. Sometimes the *land-vættir* will do that for you.

As I dreamed that night, I saw a stone figure smiling in its sadness. Don't ask me how I saw sadness. It was a dream, and sometimes you just know things in dreams. But I woke and understood, or felt I understood. Alviss the dwarf knew of many great names but knew little of *making* them. He knew, but could not know, because he had not done. Thor supposedly knew little but had the wisdom of doing.

Knowing many stories myself, I finally had some wisdom of doing. The two were not the same thing, and even my doing was not the same thing as Folki's doing. Over-matched, he had looked his death in the eye and laughed at it, knowing there would be a price to pay in that gaze. Poor swordsman or not, only a *drengr* does that. Now he fought a permanent fear of the dark as the price. That part I would not tell.

There is no better story than those who are over-matched who choose to fight anyway. And on my way back, I sometimes saw knowing nods—not at what I had told, but at what I had left out. Night terrors were not just a symptom of *draugr* fighting. Especially then, especially in the north, there were many other trolls and many other traumas. Most such trolls were nothing more than men doing evil things.

Those who survived such troll encounters often nodded as I told my story. Some lessons learned could only exist as fanciful stories. The real truth of them cut too close to the bone to speak of directly. In those nods, I recognized a knowing deeper than my own. When I saw that, I would raise my horn in honor and glory to those who were over-matched but fought anyway. Because I knew. I was there. I had just been lucky.

Not all who fight trolls survive to have their stories told. Or want to. So I carry stories and the spirits that made them live. A story might not tell exactly as it was, but if it captures the courage that was really there, the spirit of the thing is true. If there is immortality through the word-fame I create, it is in how people remember those stories. And in remembering, connections of those characters to this world are stronger long after their passing. A poet carves memory into memorable verse, hoping to preserve hard-won wisdom, the only kind that really matters.

What is a skald, other than that?

THE SAGA BEGINS

Burden to Bear is book one of Gregory Amato's Norse fantasy series *Spear of the Gods.*

When Ansgar the Skald runs into a crew of monster-hunting vikings, he finds out the hard way that **telling the Norse myths is a lot easier than living them.**

It would be insane to join them, wouldn't it? He would likely be speared or hacked to death in the first few months, and those are some of the better ways to die among this crew of maniacs . . .

. . . but the best sagas sometimes begin with the worst decisions.

Burden to Bear's opening line:

"When I first met Magnus the Red, he was sober enough to heckle me but too drunk to realize he was flirting with a witch."

If You Enjoyed This Story

Please help other people find this book.

Rate it on Goodreads and Amazon or wherever you purchased it. Review it on Bookbub and Instagram. Write about it wherever you Internet. Tell your friends—even the old-fashioned way!

It means a lot to me. It's how independent authors like me keep writing. There is no advertising more important than your ratings and reviews.

I like to keep in touch with people who like to read my work. Check out AmatoAuthor.com and sign up to receive my newsletter. You'll get project updates, cool Norse-related content, and free fiction!

About the Author

Gregory Amato made a career of selling his quill as a mercenary writer for many years. He wrote true and important things for newspapers, magazines, academia, and, for over a decade, intelligence analysis for the FBI.

Now, he writes fantasy stories based on the myths and sagas of the vikings. His fiction is often influenced by tales lost to time, usually full of high adventure, and always the sort that makes readers late to dinner.

Outside his time spent spinning yarns about vikings and wizards, he teaches Judo, brews beer, and plays DnD when he gets the chance.

Gregory lives happily with his family in the Pacific Northwest.

Sign up for updates, free fiction, and fascinating musings at **AmatoAuthor.com**!

Acknowledgments

Like the skald in my story, I did not get to where I was going by myself. Here I hope to mention most of the people who have helped me along the way.

Many thanks are due to my Alpha Readers Zepheniah Sole and Ella Grimes, who helped me make sure the major thrust of the story was on track. My Beta Readers J. Bennette Harding III, TJES, Renee Struthers, Patrick Shiflett, Ryan Connole, Eric Lonsbury, Michael Klaas, Miles Sledd, and Carrie Grimes pointed out many refinements I could make. Also, thank you all for being my first ever beta readers!

I couldn't list all the relevant scholars whose work influenced this story if I tried. As I write this, I've been engrossed in Norse myths and the history of the people who told them for almost 30 years. I owe a great debt to the hard work and dedication of many philologists, archeologists, and others.

Thank you in particular to Jackson Crawford for patiently answering questions when I thought I knew much more than I did, and for giving me the reading list that took me from motivated consumer to serious student. Tom Shippey is a fantastic educator, highly engaging writer, and also coauthor of the Hammer and the Cross series. Best Viking novels ever! Neil

Price's exhaustive work on Norse mindset and magic is some of the most interesting cross-disciplinary work I have read. Carolyne Larrington deserves special mention not just because hers is still the best translation of the Poetic Edda, and I love how she integrates modern media into her work. It is timely, and it is relevant to a vast audience.

You all, and many more, have kept alive stories that might otherwise have been forgotten. This story is is based on real myths and beliefs that are not easily pieced together. We only know as much as we do about them because of your work, and this story would not exist without you. You are the real skalds.